Too Many Toys

A CHRISTMAS STORY

Written by Betty Clark

Illustrations by Diane R. Houghton

LITTLE FRIEND PRESS

SCITUATE, MASSACHUSETTS

First U.S. edition 1996.
Printed in Hong Kong, bound
in China. Published in the
United States in 1996
by Little Friend Press,
Scituate, Massachusetts.

ISBN 0-9641285-5-1

Library of Congress
Catalog Card Number: 96-075798

LITTLE FRIEND PRESS

28 NEW DRIFTWAY

SCITUATE, MASSACHUSETTS 02066

To Jared, my grandson,
for his love and inspiration

Once upon a time,

There was a little boy,

Who had almost every game,

And almost every toy.

His toys soon filled the closet,
    The shelves and then the floor,
In the very shortest time,
    He couldn't shut the door.

He would often wonder,
Exactly what to do.

It seemed he had a thousand toys,

But he played with just a few.

Even though just yesterday,
    He'd sat on Santa's knee
And said, "I've got so many toys,
    Bring just a few to me."

He had no way of knowing that,
    Before the break of day,
He'd be asked by someone
    To give most of them away.

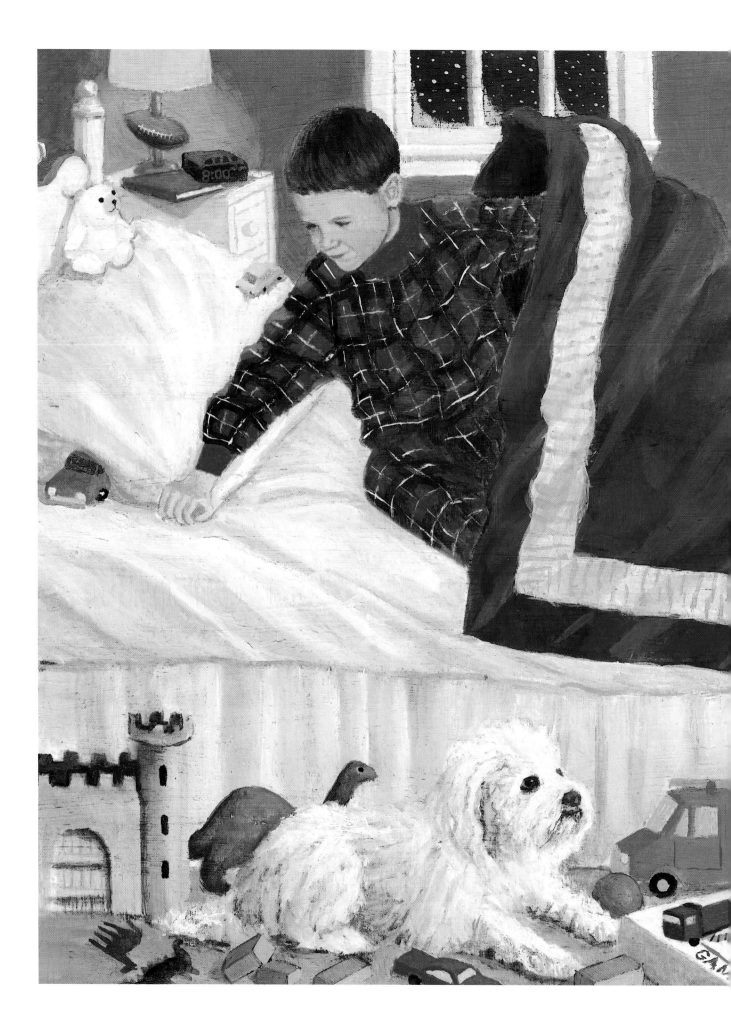

So instead of wanting more and more,
　　One snowy Christmas Eve,
He really wondered where to put
　　The toys he'd soon receive.

Then through the maze of toys
　　He stumbled to his bed,
He slipped between the blankets
　　And pulled them to his head.

For Santa, as it happened,
     Had quite a problem too.
He might just run out of toys,
     Before his work was through.

It looked as if he'd miss
     A lot of girls and boys,
Unless he acted quickly
     And found a load of toys.

Then he thought about that boy
     Who'd sat upon his knee,
And only yesterday had said,
     "Bring just a few to me."

Perhaps that boy would help him,
     Such a curious one.
We'll have to have a talk,
     To see what can be done.

So as the boy lie thinking
     Surrounded by his toys,
Something made him listen,
     He thought he heard a noise.

Was someone calling softly?
     Was that his name he heard?
He listened in the darkness,
     Saying not a word.

"It's Santa," said a voice.
    "I need to talk to you.
I have a little problem that
    You can help me through."

The boy sat up and listened,
    Surprised as he could be.
Sleepy-eyed he wondered,
    "Why is Santa calling me?"

"There's something wrong," said Santa.
"My computing must have erred.
I've surely missed some input,
And it's left me unprepared."

"I wonder if you'd mind
Giving me a hand.
I'm asking for your help.
I hope you understand."

"If we could take your extra toys,
We could make sure to see,
That every little child would have
A gift beneath a tree."

The boy could scarce believe it.
    Was it really true?
There never was a doubt,
    As to what the boy would do.

"We'll write a note to Mom and Dad,
    And tell them not to worry.
We'll tell them you're with Santa Claus,
    And tell them that we'll hurry."

With lightning speed they worked,
And before the break of day,
They had all the extra toys
loaded in the sleigh.

And on that starry night,

Skimming through the air,

Landing on the housetops,

Stopping here and there,

Were Santa and a boy,

A most unlikely pair.

And when the two were finished,

They greeted Christmas Day.

They fondly waved good-bye!

Then Santa pulled away.

The boy soon fell asleep.
    The happiest of boys,
With not so many games,
    And not so many toys.

He didn't have the clutter.
    And he didn't have the mess.
Yet in their place, he'd found
    A strange new happiness.

For there is joy in sharing.
    He knew it now because,
One snowy Christmas Eve,
    He'd helped Santa Claus.

And though he didn't know it,
   In the morning he would see,
Something very special
   Hanging on the Christmas tree.

A shiny gold ornament.

    Showing Santa in a sleigh

Beside a little boy

    Who gave his toys away.